Popsy in Versailles

BY
Betsy Walker

Illustrations by
LEAH GONZALES

Author: Betsy Walker
Illustrator: Leah Gonzales
Editor: Aura Rose Bolinger
Design and Layout: Ann Lowe

For Kathy
In Fond Memory of Popsy

Acknowledgements

IT HAS BEEN A LONG JOURNEY to write this little book. Many people encouraged me and worked with me, keeping me in forward motion. This was especially important during those times when I feared that technical writing was all I could do. Flannery Davis – if not for you, this story would still be sitting unfinished in some obscure corner at the back of my "Documents" folder. Thank you for encouraging me to write just for the pure joy of the process. Aura Rose Bolinger – my dear riding friend! I am so grateful for your editing expertise. You helped me to turn my "Betsy Speak" manner of writing into acceptable English, which makes Sam and Ebie Walker very relieved and proud. Leah Gonzales, just when I feared that illustrations might not ever get drawn, you stepped up to the plate and helped to bring a whimsical and colorful vision to my story. Thank you for putting up with this anxious newbie author who had no clue how to work with an illustrator. Ann Lowe – my designer and layout expert. Our meeting by chance at lunch was perfect timing. It was one of those encounters that leaves me wondering if maybe Popsy herself is not watching over this process and guiding the events.

Many friends read my story, told me they enjoyed it, encouraged me to keep going – you are too numerous to name, but I hope you know who you are. I thank you for giving me the courage to create.

Table of Contents

Mamina in the Morning

ONCE UPON A TIME, in the fifteenth arrondissement of Paris, on Avenue Felix-Faure, in a quiet residential apartment, there lived a truly magnificent cat. Popsy was a lovely, long-haired calico. She had green eyes and a regal dappling of gold, black, and white all over her body. She had soft, long luxurious fur and her tail ended in a magnificent POOF! She was, indeed, très élégante!

One midmorning in March, Popsy awoke from her after-breakfast nap to find that it was still and quiet all through the apartment. Listening extra carefully, she noted that there was also no sound of rain—a great sign. No rain meant outdoor time! Before rising, she opened her eyes just the teeniest bit to look around the apartment. Was anyone else here? She loved to awaken slowly, with no disturbances. Everything seemed quiet; all she heard were the sounds of Mamina busy in the kitchen. So she s-t-r-e-t-c-h-e-d herself oh-so-gracefully in her basket, first one leg, then another, reaching as far as she could, right through the tips of her toes. Then she arched her back and flexed her nails one by one, admiring their sharpness and length. "Oh, my," she thought to herself, "aren't they pretty? And so effective! Those nasty city creatures down in the garden certainly keep their distance from me, don't they? And mice? Not one has dared to show up in our quatier in two years. With these nails, my dreamy green eyes, and my lovely fur coat, I certainly am the queen of the courtyard garden. Maybe even the queen of the whole arrondissement—yes!"

With a quick pop-pat, she hopped out of her basket onto the floor and trotted off to the kitchen. Hmm . . . what was Mamina doing in there?

"Well hello there, my dear petit Chaton," crooned Mamina. Picking Popsy up, she gave her a little tickle under the chin and stroked the lovely long fur down her back. With a sigh, Popsy endured this attention. So frivolous. Such an invasion of her personal space. "Ah well," she thought. "My human is really quite nice. After all, she does feed me. And when that noisy human boy Charles is here, she stops him from teasing me. Yes, I guess that I can put up with this for just a moment. But then on to business—I must go outside today!"

After just a minute of Mamina's attention, Popsy wriggled out of her arms, jumped down, and ran to the front door. "Please, Mamina," she meowed. "Open this door! Let's go *outside!*"

Mamina chuckled. She knew her kitty very well, and she understood that all cats need time in gardens. After all, Popsy had a job to do; she was the Watch Kitty of the apartment garden. Today, after weeks of gray skies and drizzling rain, the clouds were finally gone, the rain had stopped, the sky was blue, and the weather was warm and sunny. But in Paris, you never knew how long this would last. So, thought Popsy, "Quand il fait un temps si beaux, il faut en profiter!" She must take advantage of this weather! It really was the most perfect kind of day for Popsy to patrol outside; so Mamina lifted her into her arms, opened the stairwell door, and descended to the foyer. There she opened the apartment-building door to the outside, carried Popsy over to the low garden wall, and set her gently on it.

Suddenly Popsy was FREE!

"Now Popsy, you be a good kitty," said Mamina. "I'll come down to get you in an hour. In the meantime, have fun and be sure that you stay out of the street!"

"See you later, Mamina!" With a quick meow, Popsy was off to resharpen her nails on the garden tree because, as everybody knows, one's nails can never be too sharp. It felt oh-so-good to sink her nails into the tree bark, flex her toes, and pull up and down and back and forth. Yes, this was certainly one of the most satisfying feelings that Popsy knew. It was just . . . perfect.

"Today is off to such a good start," she thought. "Today will be a grand day."

The Truck

AFTER A MINUTE OR TWO of nail sharpening, Popsy dropped her paws back to the ground and took a good look around. Was there anything new in the courtyard? Some crocuses had poked their noses up out of the dirt. "That's good," she thought. Mamina loved flowers and had planted these herself. It would make her happy to see them emerging, and their growth would be helped a lot by the sunny day. Popsy walked over to give them a sniff; no perfume yet.

Her attention shifted to the door of the concierge's office to see if there was any activity. Popsy always enjoyed her time in the garden best when she had the courtyard to herself. It was much more fun when there were no nosy humans trying to pet her. Happily, everything seemed quiet that morning; no deliveries, no postmen, no visitors, no sound of voices. Nobody about at all, really. Satisfied that she was alone in the courtyard, she decided to check out the garden perimeter.

When Popsy had first visited the garden, she had noticed that a mouse family had taken up housekeeping in the garden wall. There was a hole, just mouse-sized, where she'd had to sit and wait for hours on end to get a glimpse of them. What patience that had required! Those mice had been very careful, and for days Popsy had only been able to smell them, with just an occasional sight of a whisker or tip of a mouse tail. She'd sat guard during every garden visit for a full week. Finally they had moved away. She could tell that they were no longer there; the scent of them ebbed away a bit more each day. Popsy was a little disappointed that she didn't actually get to eat one, but she was pleased that she had met her first challenge as Garden Watch Kitty so effectively.

Ever since then, Popsy checked that hole whenever she visited the garden, just to be sure that no mouse or other creature had decided to test their luck in this garden and move in. They'd better watch out if they did! Now, Popsy silently sneaked up to the edge of the wall and peeked over so that she could just see the edge of the mouse hole. Everything was still and quiet, but she decided to wait for a minute, just in case a mouse was hiding inside.

As she waited, her tummy grumbled a bit. Mamina had fed her breakfast this morning, but Popsy had decided not to eat it. This was a game she played with Mamina sometimes. Popsy would refuse to eat, and then Mamina would open three or four different flavored cans of food, trying to please her. Popsy enjoyed watching all that extra effort. But this morning, Mamina hadn't seemed to notice that Popsy hadn't eaten, so the trick hadn't worked, and now Popsy was a bit hungry. "Oh, I do hope that there *is* a mouse in there today! Now that would make a delightful breakfast indeed!" Popsy had never actually tasted mouse, but she was sure that it must be a delicious flavor. Not as wonderful as shrimp—<u>nothing</u> could be that good—but she was sure that mouse must be a very close second.

Suddenly her nose picked up her favorite scent. She lifted her head up and wrinkled her nose back and forth, sniffing to be sure she was not mistaken. Yes! She was certain! She smelled . . . SHRIMP! How could that be possible? Where could that be coming from? Excitedly, she looked around, trying to pinpoint the source.

Her gaze landed on a blue truck parked outside the courtyard gate. On the side of the truck were painted pictures of—yes—shrimp! Popsy's whole body trembled in excitement—a seafood delivery truck! Was the ocean in that truck? Popsy knew a few things about oceans from her trips with the family to Corsica. But how did a truck carry sea creatures? The smell of those shrimp was so enticing that Popsy became lightheaded with hunger. Oh, how she wished that truck were inside the courtyard gate, not on the forbidden outside! How she would love to peek inside and grab one tasty little morsel of shrimp. Stolen shrimp always tasted best.

Popsy walked over to the gate, poked her head through the bars, and gazed longingly at the truck. She saw that the door to the back of the truck was open. Inside there were boxes, stacked one on top of another. "Hmm . . . I wonder if there is a little bit of ocean in each of those boxes. Are the shrimp swimming in there? Are they playing with oysters and scallops?"

Surely Mamina wouldn't mind if Popsy hopped through for just a second. As a matter of a fact, Mamina wouldn't even have to know. Of course she couldn't have guessed that a seafood truck would be parked so near. Nobody could reasonably expect Popsy to follow a rule when such tempting delicacies were so close by.

Before she even realized it herself, Popsy had stepped through the bars of the gate onto the sidewalk pavement. With three easy leaps, she was next to the truck, peering up at the opening and all those boxes. The smell of shrimp was so strong now that her head felt like it was spinning. She felt a little afraid of this new place. But oh my goodness, SHRIMP! Right here in front of her! "Okay," she thought to herself, "take a deep breath. Un . . . deux . . . trois . . . allez-oop!" and she jumped up into the truck.

As soon as Popsy landed in the back of the truck, she crouched, looking around cautiously, just to be sure there were no dogs or little boys hiding in there. She looked up at all the boxes piled in stacks in the back of the truck. "Oh my goodness, I'm actually surrounded by shrimp! This must be a truck to heaven!" she sighed. Slowly she crept up to one box that was over to the side. She slipped into a space between this box and the pile towering next to it. As she sniffed and licked around the corners of the box, the aroma was so strong she could actually taste the shrimp. Desperate to get inside this carton, she picked at a loose flap with her ever-so-sharp-and-long nails. There! An edge of the flap came loose, and—yes!—there was a small piece of shrimp tail poking out of the hole she had made! She grabbed it with her teeth and gave a good yank. POP! Out came a small baby shrimp. Popsy sank her teeth into the shrimp and started to purr as the delicious flavor filled her mouth, tickled her tongue, and trickled down her throat. With a gulp, she swallowed the shrimp and looked carefully at the hole she had made to see if there was another shrimp visible that she might pull out.

BANG! With a sudden crashing sound, the world went dark. Popsy's heart jumped into her throat, beating wildly. The door! Someone had closed the truck door! She was trapped!

Pierre-Yves

PIERRE-YVES SLAMMED DOWN the door of his fish delivery truck and walked back to get into the driver's seat. "Zut alors!" he muttered. What a long morning this was becoming! Initially he'd hoped to get all of his deliveries taken care of early so that he could make it a short day and get home in time to take his daughter, Sybile, to her favorite park to play and ride her bicycle. It had been weeks since he'd been able to spend time with her, and last night he'd promised her that he would set aside time for just the two of them.

But just now his boss, the fat and smelly fish man, Maurice LeGros, had rung him on his cell phone and announced that Pierre-Yves would have to make an urgent delivery run to the Château at Versailles. What? The Château at Versailles? That was not his territory! Apparently, the shrimp that had been intended for this evening's soiree at the château had been left unrefrigerated overnight and had spoiled horribly. Blech!

9

The executive chef of the Château at Versailles knew that Monsieur LeGros was the only fish man in all of Paris who could be relied on to make such a delivery at the last minute like this. Yes, he was fat; yes, he was smelly; but his seafood was the best. So, as the fish man's most reliable driver, Pierre-Yves would have to deliver all his shrimp to the château; shrimp that originally had been meant for the various fish merchants in this section of Paris, the fifteenth arrondissement. Pierre-Yves ground his teeth in frustration. Today of all days! This would totally throw off his schedule and delay his rounds by at least two hours, if not more. Not to mention the annoyed attitudes he would encounter with his regular customers when he came back next week. He knew that the local merchants preferred to buy their shrimp from him, and with no delivery today, they would have none to sell. He would have a lot of explaining to do.

He climbed into the cab of his truck and slammed the door. He then turned on the engine and drove through the Place Balard, under the train tracks, and on toward the entrance of the Peripherique, the highway that wrapped around Paris. Maybe he'd be lucky and miss the morning rush of traffic. Speeding up a bit, his truck bumped along the street. He could hear some of the boxes of shrimp being jostled around in the back, but he pressed the accelerator harder as he swore under his breath, "Tant pis!" He did not care if the boxes were jostled; he was in a hurry!

Pierre-Yves made it to the entrance of the highway without encountering too much traffic; that was a great relief. Fortunately he only had to go a short distance before his exit toward the château. He proceeded with relative ease. Maybe the gods were not against him that day after all. But he suspected that once he got to the château, he could be kept waiting in the courtyard for some time. So he continued to speed along in his haste to get there as soon as he could, swerving and jockeying for position through the lanes of traffic. If the boxes in the back got a little banged up, so be it!

Finally, after leaving the highway and driving through the Parisian suburbs, Pierre-Yves arrived in the town of Versailles and turned onto the Avenue de Paris. As annoyed and angry as he might have been with the inconvenience of this task, he had to admit to himself that he always loved the view of the château from here. This avenue, lined with tall, leafy sycamores, led to the main courtyard entrance to the château. It never failed to fill his heart with national pride. As he approached the grand entrance to the château, with the majestic statue of Louis XIV atop his mighty steed just outside the gates, it was easy for him to pretend that he was driving a horse-drawn carriage with a noble duchess inside on her way to a rendezvous with the king, instead of an old and somewhat beat-up Renault truck full of seafood. Ah, Pierre-Yves was really a romantic Frenchman in his heart! Once he arrived at the main gates, he drove around the Place d'Armee toward the side of the château. There should be an entrance to a courtyard where Monsieur LeGros had assured him there would be someone waiting to receive the precious cargo.

Driving carefully now, he found the entryway that Monsieur LeGros had described. He pulled into the side courtyard where there were lots of other delivery trucks, all unloading their contents into the waiting arms of catering staff. There was a great deal of hustle and bustle as harried workers ran back and forth between the delivery trucks and the side door of the château. The courtyard was full of the smells and colors of a grand event in the making. Flow-ers and bread and huge wheels of cheese and caviar and pâté and bottles of wine and champagne were all being rushed inside. Two kitchen managers marched around officiously barking orders to their assistants. Everyone seemed very anxious, and there was a feeling of great urgency in the air.

"Probably just a dinner for a lot of overfed, self-important politicians," thought Pierre-Yves. All he wanted was to unload his shrimp and get out of there, but he knew there would be paperwork and other official details to confirm before he would be done and ready to go.

He pulled up behind a bread truck and turned off his engine. As he opened his door and stepped out into the courtyard, one of the attendants rushed up to him with a look of immense relief on his face. Was this perhaps the person who had forgotten to put away the shrimp last night? Pierre-Yves thought probably so.

"Oh, monsieur, it is you who have brought the shrimp, yes? Please say that it is you!" As PierreYves nodded his affirmation, the young attendant heaved a sigh, and a smile relaxed the features of his worried face.

"Not so fast!" a voice bellowed from behind Pierre-Yves's truck. "Let's just take a look at those shrimp before we unload anything from this truck." It was, of course, the voice of one of the kitchen managers, and Pierre-Yves was now a little worried about the fact that he'd allowed the boxes to get so bounced around on his way over here. Taking a deep breath, he stepped toward the back of the truck, unlocked the handle, and slid the door up, hoping that the cases were not in too much disarray. As the door rolled up an unidentifiable orange, white, and black object burst out of the truck and hurtled past his head at lightning speed. It was as if a cannonball was shot full force right past him!

Where Am I Now?

POPSY CATAPULTED OUT OF THE TRUCK, hit the ground running, and dashed as quickly as she could under the nearest object that offered her any cover. She scrunched herself into the tiniest ball she could manage, clenched her eyes shut, and began an uncontrollable shivering. What a ride she had just endured! Slipping and sliding around in the back of that truck in total darkness, she'd had to guess where the cases of shrimp were and how to keep out of their way as the truck careened through the streets. What relief she'd felt when it finally came to rest! But then the unfamiliar voices of so many humans made her realize that she had journeyed to some new place where she wouldn't know anybody. She wasn't in the fifteenth arrondissement anymore—her gut told her that she had entered some strange land. What was she going to do?

In the darkness, she had figured that getting away from the shrimp cases and out of the truck was her greatest priority. So she had cautiously inched her way as close to the back of the truck as she dared, and when she heard the driver unlock the door, she poised herself for a great leap. When the door slid open, she burst forth, just barely missing the head of the driver on her way out.

Having landed under a delivery van, Popsy kept her eyes tightly closed and tried to get control of her breathing. "Deep breaths, Popsy," she whispered to herself in an attempt to calm down. She was hyperventilating terribly, which just increased her shivering. So she took one deep breath . . . exhale . . . another deep breath . . . exhale. This seemed to help, so she continued the quiet exercise for a minute or two until she could feel her heart rate slow down.

With her attention off her pounding heart, Popsy's nose caught a scent that was totally unexpected. She sniffed again, concentrating on the odors of this courtyard. They were not at all what she would have guessed. She knew what cars and trucks and exhaust smelled like. She often smelled those heavy odors from the traffic in the streets that surrounded Mamina's courtyard. The whole time she was in that seafood delivery truck, she'd been aware of the underlying stink of the truck's oily metallic odor. Now, quite suddenly, all of that was gone. Instead, her nose was assaulted by the strong odor of other animals in the courtyard.

The sounds in the air were different too. No longer did she hear engines revving and truck doors slamming. Instead she could hear . . . feet? Big footsteps were clomping all around her. What was this? Ever so slowly she opened one eye just the teeniest bit. Peeking out from under this hiding place, this . . . horse cart? Wait! What happened to the truck she'd hidden under? How did she get under a horse-drawn cart? Hers eyes both popped fully open now, and she gasped and caught her breath in shock. The courtyard was still filled with deliverymen and their wares, but there was not a single truck anywhere! Instead the deliveries were all being unloaded from wooden carts pulled by horses who stood stomping their feet and swishing their tails.

Oh, mon Dieu!! Where was this place? What were these carts? How did horses suddenly appear? Or maybe the real question was *when* was this?

A Mouse, A Mouse!

POPSY LAID LOW under the wooden delivery cart as she watched the hustle and bustle of the deliveries before her. All the same activities of unloading food supplies were underway as when she had first arrived. But it was all changed. Now, not just the vehicles were different; the clothing worn by these people were totally unfamiliar too.

Popsy had always been of the opinion that the clothes worn by humans seemed a paltry substitute for a luxurious coat of fur, but at least the things that Mamina and her family wore served their purpose in a streamlined sort of way. Their slacks allowed for economy of movement, and their t-shirts and blouses covered them well enough without getting in the way of activity. But the clothing she saw before her now seemed so excessive—blousy shirts with big puffy sleeves; long, full skirts on the women; tall, starched hats with feathery plumes on the men. All this appeared to Popsy as nothing more than vanity. Of course, Popsy was not unfamiliar with vanity;

she liked to strut her stuff a bit herself. But *her* vanity was justified—this was simply silly!

As time passed, Popsy became more and more aware of her hunger. She'd been feeling its pangs for hours now, and at this point she was starting to care less about maintaining her hiding place than about finding something to eat. Suddenly, out of the corner of her eye, she saw a flash of brown fur dart into an open door in the side of the château. Aha! Was it a mouse? What better time than the present for her to get that first real taste!

Popsy leapt to the chase and bolted through the doorway after her prey. She got there just in time to see the tip of a tail disappear around a corner. She charged in hot pursuit after it. The mouse ran for dear life down a hallway, Popsy gaining on it with every stride. Oh yes, Popsy could imagine the taste of mouse filling her mouth and her tummy as she ran. Then, in the blink of an eye, the mouse popped into a tiny hole in the wall. As quickly as he had appeared, the rodent was gone. Disappeared. Darn! So near, and yet so far!

The Kitchen

EEKING BACK AROUND the corner she'd just rounded, Popsy realized that she had run straight through the room where the feast was being prepared for the evening's gala event. A room full of food! Her tummy grumbled so loudly now she was sure everyone there must have been able to hear it. But nobody paid attention to her. They were all busily engaged with the creation of dozens of spectacular dishes of food. There were platters with whole wild boars and pheasants, cheeses, caviar, fish, and—yes!— there were her cases of shrimp coming in the door! (She did feel that they were <u>her</u> shrimp, having taken her life into her paws to travel here with them.) Fruit carved and assembled to look like swans and pastries shaped like stars from the heavens graced magnificent silver trays. Huge vessels of wine accompanied ice sculptures of rearing horses.

Wow! Mamina never put on a dinner like this!

The room was buzzing with activity. Knives were flashing in the afternoon sunlight that streamed through the windows; the sounds of chopping were mixed into voices that called to each other across the room.

"Pass me that bowl. That one, right there!"

"I need more olive oil. Where did the bottle go? Did you take it?"

"Eh! Toi! Move from my space, I am carving here!"

As the knives whisked through the air, small tidbits of food trimmings flew after them, landing mostly in pails but occasionally landing on the floor beneath the tables.

It was these stray pieces that caught Popsy's attention. Did she dare? She must! Ravenous with hunger now, Popsy spied a large morsel of fat on the floor under one of the tables. She waited until the man carving the edges of that particular roasted boar was leaning over to adjust the decorative arrangement of vegetables around the edge of his platter. She tore across the room as fast as her feet would carry her, snapped up the meat in passing, swung around in an arc, and continued running until she safely returned to the corner of the hallway.

Unable to contain herself, she chomped and chewed this tough piece of rejected gristle noisily. "Mm-hng-unng," she moaned, almost singing as the flavor of the oily rind filled her mouth and began to dribble down into the empty cavity of her belly. Tipping her head to the side, she chewed the sinewy rind of boar using her back teeth. It took some long minutes to eat, but what minutes of bliss! Yes, it is true that stolen food tastes the very best!

Once this piece was eaten, Popsy felt much better but still hungry. Emboldened by her success, she peeked out again to see if she could spy another available tidbit to pinch. There! She saw another chunk of fat fly through the air and land on the floor, just missing the trash bucket. Once again, Popsy darted forward. Just as she was closing her jaws on her target, she heard one of the women yell, "Hey! Look out! What is that? A rat? It is the biggest one I've ever seen!"

Oh no! She'd been seen! She was caught! Where could she go? Without even thinking, Popsy jumped quickly to her right. Instead of circling back to her hiding spot, she had hopped behind a white tablecloth that was draped over a table roulante. She hunkered down behind the cloth, held her breath, and waited. Would she be safe? Or would they grab her and throw her out the door?

"Eh, ma vieille! You are always seeing things! There is nothing there! I think maybe you had a little bit too much to drink last night, no? Just put your mind back on those flowers and do not worry about les rats!"

Whew—another near miss! Popsy knew that she had some lucky stars to thank this day. She heaved a big (but silent) sigh and started to chew the gristle still held in her mouth. Quietly this time, she gnawed her way through the piece of fat until it was all safely in her tummy. She felt much better but decidedly thirsty. Now, what to do about that?

Looking around, she realized that next to her on this bottom shelf of the table roulante were bowls of water with slices of lemon in them. Oh yes, those would do nicely! How perfect was this? Slowly, she turned to face the bowl nearest to her and, as silently as she could, she lapped up some of the lemon water. Yum! It was very good! She kept drinking until it was all gone, with just lemon rinds and a few cubes of ice left at the bottom of the bowl.

Popsy gave a quiet but very satisfying little burp. Ah!

Juliette

DURING THIS FIRST DAY working in the kitchen of the château, Juliette did her best to focus on the task at hand. It was her job to help the master ice carver, Edgard Le Maître de la Glace. As he busily cut away at the huge ice block, removing all the bits and pieces that did not resemble a rearing horse, chunks and shavings of ice flew around the table in a furious storm. Juliette's job was to follow along with a small whisk broom and clear away the ice shavings so that the ice master would have a clear view of his work at all times. She had to quickly brush the ice pieces away before they stuck to the sculpture. Her hands were so cold! Red and wet and frigid, her fingers could barely even feel the broom handle that she clutched for dear life.

The ice master was a kind man, but proved to be impatient when in the throes of creation. At first it seemed that Juliette could do nothing right. Le Maître kept complaining that she was not fast enough, or she was in his way, or she was scratching his masterpiece with the bristles of her broom. But after a while a rhythm seemed to develop between them, and the complaints died away. Then she and Le Maître fell into compatible movement—almost like a dance, she thought—as they moved in harmony around his worktable.

Juliette was happy to be working in the kitchen. After two years of working as a chambermaid, she was relieved not to have to empty the disgusting, stinky, sloppy chamber pots any more. Ugh—that had been the worst job in the world! Working in the kitchen was an opportunity that did not come to a chambermaid every day, and she knew that if she did a good job here, she might be able to count on this improved station in life for a long time. So she was most anxious to please Edgard Le Maître de la Glace. He was an influential figure and could make or break this opportunity for her.

Glancing over at Le Maître, Juliette noticed that he had stopped carving. He stood quietly, with his arms folded in front of his chest, and then he began to walk in slow, even steps around his worktable. Eyeing the sculpture, he would tap gently with his knife here, scrape a thin line there, until finally he nodded with pleasure. "Fini!" he exclaimed. It was done!

Just then, one of the cooks nearby shrieked something about seeing a rat. "Oh, gross!" thought Juliette, looking around nervously. She saw Le Maître glance over toward the cook on the other side of the room, and upon seeing who had cried out, he retorted, "Eh, ma vieille! You are always seeing things! There is nothing there! I think maybe you had a little bit too much to drink last night, no? Just put your mind back on those flowers and do not worry about les rats!"

Turning back, he said with great dignity, "Alright, Juliette, we are now ready to present this masterpiece to Le Roi! He insists on having his own private champagne in his boudoir before he joins his guests in the ballroom. Go get that table roulante with the champagne and caviar. Mon ami, Vincent, will help me to carry this tray with the sculpture. Vas vite!"

Juliette glanced across the room and saw the table roulante covered with a white tablecloth. On top of it she saw a bottle of the finest champagne, chilling in an iced silver bowl. Next to the champagne were crystal dishes of caviar with lemon slices and thick cream; spoons made of mother-of-pearl, gently wrapped in lace napkins, lay beside them.

Pushing the table roulante over toward Le Maître, Juliette felt its weight. It was a little bit heavier than she expected, and it seemed to jiggle, as though something were out of balance. She stopped and looked over everything carefully. She must not make a mistake tonight; she would be in the presence of Le Roi Louis XIV—the Sun King! This was such an honor! She hastily glanced behind the tablecloth and saw the small bowls of lemon water lined up on the bottom shelf. Everything seemed to be as it should. Tidying her hair with both hands, Juliette smoothed out her dress, took a deep breath, and followed Edgard Le Maître de la Glace out of the room.

She soon realized that she would need to rush if she meant to keep up with Le Maître. He and Vincent seemed to be walking as fast as they could, carrying the tray with the ice sculpture between them. It looked terribly awkward having to travel sideways and still keep the tray balanced. She knew the tray must be top-heavy with that tall sculpture of the rearing horse on it. Juliette could see a look of concentration and concern on Le Maître's face. He must be anxious to get the sculpture to the boudoir of the king before it began to melt and lose its fine definition. That must be it!

They proceeded quickly but quietly, getting closer and closer to the king's boudoir, footmen opening doors for them as they passed from one room to the next. Juliette knew the way well; she had cleaned all of these rooms many times. But she had never before been allowed to enter when they were in use by their rightful inhabitants.

The further they travelled from the kitchen the more elegant the rooms became. Each successive chamber had more and more magnificent crystal chandeliers, portraits of royalty in elaborate gold leaf frames, highly polished parquet floors, and walls covered by tapestries of silk. All of this was bathed in the golden light of the late afternoon sun as it poured in through the towering high windows.

It was breathtaking.

Finally they passed through the king's apartment and arrived at the closed door of the king's bedchamber. There stood a guard, eyeing Le Maître and the ice sculpture suspiciously. He made no move to open the door, but merely raised one eyebrow with a hint of derision.

"Hurry, you fool!" exclaimed Le Maître. "The king awaits his champagne, caviar, and ice sculpture! He always enjoys his private degustation before a grand event. What are you waiting for? Do you wish for the ice to melt and the champagne to warm while you waste our time? If that happens, I can assure you, the king will know whose fault it is!"

Juliette suppressed a smile. Edgard Le Maître de la Glace certainly did not let anyone stand in his way! With the ringing tones of his admonishment still lingering in the air, the guard bowed, reached forward to the door handle, and, with an air of great solemnity, swept open the entrance to the king's bedchamber.

Juliette felt her hands begin to tremble. Up until this moment, she had been so concerned about keeping up the pace with Le Maître that she hadn't allowed herself to become nervous. It had been a bit of a trick to push this table roulante from room to room so quickly without letting the bowls slide about. It had taken all of her concentration not to let anything spill.

But now here she was. Glancing ahead as she proceeded, she saw *him* just beyond the two doors. Yes, it really was him—the Sun King! There he was, sitting on a chair off to the side of his bed, watching and waiting for the delivery of his champagne. A look of annoyance showed on his face. He sighed and fanned himself, rolling his eyes up toward the ceiling and shaking his head as if in disgust.

Following Edgard Le Maître de la Glace, Juliette entered the king's boudoir. Just inside the door, she pushed the table roulante a few more steps toward the king and stopped. She stepped back, lowered her head, and curtsied as deeply as her knees would allow.

She dared not look up unbidden, so she held her curtsy and kept her head lowered. What would happen now? Would Le Maître actually speak to the king? Would the king respond?

Suddenly the king burst into a peal of laughter. Oh my goodness, what was it? Had her hairpins slipped? Was her clothing absurd? Why was he laughing?

"Le Maître, bravo! I love this rearing horse! Ha ha! My wife thinks that I spend too much time with horses as it is, but now wait until I tell her that there is one in my bedroom—a wild rearing one at that! Well done! This will make for the grandest joke of the evening. Oh, I am very pleased indeed! Bien fait, mon vieux!"

Juliette glanced sideways and saw that Le Maître beamed with pride. He gestured for her to stand up straight but to remain silent, which she did. He then said, "Oh, Your Majesty, you honor me so! I am

but your humble ice artist and only work to serve you and to please
you. If this small effort of mine should bring you joy, then my day is
complete. Allow me to pour your first glass of champagne."

Le Maître opened the bottle with a resounding pop, poured
some champagne into a glass, and served it to the king. He then mo-
tioned to Juliette that she should begin bowing and backing out of the
room. He followed her, also walking backward and bowing as he went.
With their final steps out of the bedchamber, the door closed.

The Royal Bedchamber

AT LAST, the table had stopped moving! In order to stay on, Popsy had splayed out all four of her legs and sunk her ever-so-sharp-and-long nails into the wood of the shelf beneath her. The journey through the château had not been as long as her ride in the seafood truck that morning, but she had been so close to being exposed that it felt like hours had passed instead of minutes while she clung to the shelf in this position. The vibration of the wheels beneath her had tickled right up into her newly filled tummy, and she had worried that she might be sick if the movement did not stop.

But stop it had.

Initially there was no sound. Then she heard laughter; loud, ringing laughter. Then words were exchanged between two men. Then a loud popping noise was followed by the sound of a liquid being poured into a glass; this was followed by the sound of doors closing. Popsy could hear the human who remained in the room move over to the side. She heard the feet of a chair move slightly as the man sat down. Finally there was only silence.

Popsy waited and tried her best to catch her breath and still her wildly beating heart. She remained hunkered down on the table roulante shelf, curtained off from the room by the white tablecloth covering the cart. For now, she was unseen. But how long would that last?

Minutes passed. This human was very quiet; Popsy thought perhaps he had fallen asleep. If that was the case, maybe she could get off of this cart and find someplace more comfortable to hide. She'd have to peek into the room so she could assess her situation. As slowly as she could, she turned around on the shelf, doing her best to make no sound. Then she poked just the tip of her nose out from behind the tablecloth. She sniffed to see if she could smell any danger. No, there was no scent of little boys or dogs. The tip of her tail twitched. Stop that! She concentrated on keeping motionless. She repeated the breathing mantra that she had devised that morning in the château courtyard: "Take a deep breath . . . exhale." She repeated this over and over. It was a good calming technique.

More minutes passed; still only silence. She was becoming very curious. Who was this human, and what was he doing? She inched just a teeny bit more toward the edge of the shelf and poked her nose a little further out. The tablecloth pushed aside, and she was then able to peek toward the windows. "Oh! Mon Dieu," she gasped in panic.

He was looking right at her.

Exposed

THEIR EYES MET, and Popsy froze. She barely dared to even breathe now. What would this human do? She had made it so far through this arduous day without being caught. But now she found herself face-to-face with a stranger who might hurt her or throw her out or . . . who knew what he might do?

Popsy took a moment to look carefully at this man. His appearance was bizarre, unlike that of anyone she'd ever seen before. He wore a white silk shirt that burst forth in billowy ruffles of lace from the sleeves and lapels of a royal blue waistcoat. Instead of pants, he wore stockings that were embroidered from the thighs to the ankles, showing off short yet muscular legs. He sported bright red shoes with high heels. This seemed very strange to Popsy; Mamina and her daughters were the only people Popsy had ever seen with high heels.

Above all, Popsy could not stop staring at this human's hair. It was like a mountain that towered high above his head in a huge mass of dark ringlets that fell past his shoulders and down to his waist. There

was so much of this hair that it appeared like another garment itself.
What kind of man was this?

This human, this "king" continued to look at her as he said, "Well,
petit Chaton, who are you? What are you doing in the bedchamber of
a king? Do you even know who I am? My courtiers are all afraid of me,
but here you arrive, uninvited, a brazen little thing indeed!"

As the man spoke, Popsy kept her gaze locked with his. She had
learned that a human's truest nature showed in the eyes. This man, this
"king," as he called himself, had eyes that seemed to sparkle. His eye-
brows lifted slightly, as if in laughter, and a smile played at the corners
of his mouth. Was he mocking her? How dare he!

Yes, she *was* brazen—Popsy knew that about herself. And she
was not sure that she wanted to strike up a friendship with some silly
human who looked like a character off of Mamina's television set. She
found it difficult to take this man seriously. He looked too much like
a cartoon to be believable.

With a confidence that surprised even herself, Popsy jumped
off the cart and immediately turned her back on this man. She strutted away, waving her tail at this "king" with the most dismissive flip
of her hips that she could muster. If he wanted to be her friend, he
would have to earn it. Even as an intruder, she was after all, très
élégante. She had travelled far today, meeting many challenges along
the way. She was brave, intelligent, and beautiful. She would not
tolerate being teased.

As she walked away from the king, Popsy could not help but
marvel at the décor of this room. Everywhere she looked there were
rich deep colors: in the carpet, in the small sculptures on the gilt tables,
and in the tapestries and oil paintings that hung on the walls. The bed

was covered with a quilt embroidered in gold and had a mountain of pillows at the head. Magnificent fabric, draped from four points high above the bed, tumbled to either side in folds of deep red and gold.

Now this was a bed Popsy imagined would be perfect for an afternoon nap! She would have to give that a try, and soon. She was tired after her long day, and the thought of a nap made her yawn.

"Eh, ma petite amie, I am going to step outside to enjoy this late afternoon light. It is truly golden light, which is my favorite color. It is the color of royalty! Would you like to enjoy a little fresh air with me in the garden?"

Popsy glanced over toward the king, and saw that he had opened one of the tall glass doors to the outside. This made her think that a quick visit to the garden was not a bad idea at all. She'd not had a "private moment" since early that morning, and this might be a perfect opportunity.

So, deciding that she could teach this human a lesson in humility outdoors as well as indoors, she trotted over to him and passed through the doorway. Popsy felt regal having him open and hold the door for her, and she held her head and tail high as she strutted past.

The king was right; the light in the garden was lovely. The golden glow poured over her back and shoulders, its molten warmth seeping into her muscles. It made her realize that she was very stiff from having spent so much of the day in various stressed and frozen positions— first in the back of the fish delivery truck, then under the wagon in the courtyard, then on the table roulante. It had been a long day of little movement.

The air smelled deliciously sweet. There were roses everywhere; red, yellow, white, and even peach roses surrounded them. Popsy walked over and inhaled the heady perfume of a dark red rose. "Oh, Mamina's daughter, Alex, would love this," she thought. "I know that Alex prides herself on her roses." She then sniffed around the dirt at the base of the rosebush. It had a moist, rich aroma that was most inviting. This was a perfect private place.

When she was done, she turned back to look at the king. He was seated at an outdoor table, quietly sipping his champagne and smiling at her. He pointed to a chair next to him and tapped it gently. "Come, ma petite amie, join me here at the table. I have brought you a dish of my caviar. Have you ever tasted caviar?"

"Caviar?" Popsy wondered. "What is caviar?" Curious, she hopped up to see what the king was talking about. Immediately, she caught a scent of the sea. How divine! This was a scent similar to shrimp but more pungent. A scallop-shaped crystal dish sat on the chair next to her. It was filled with hundreds of tiny, moist black pearls that glistened in the golden light.

Popsy leaned toward the dish and took a careful bite. Oh. Mon. Dieu! Heaven, she was in heaven! Her mouth instantly filled with a deep and rich salty flavor, as though she had bitten into the ocean itself. This rivaled even the taste of shrimp, something she'd never thought possible. It was a stronger, more commanding flavor—just delicious! "Well," thought Popsy, "this King might have a foolish appearance, but clearly he understands good food! Perhaps he did not mean to mock me before. He is most generous with his caviar. Maybe he could be my friend after all. I suppose that I can forgive him for his earlier behavior."

Closing her eyes to better savor this new delicacy, Popsy continued eating the delicious pearls until the dish was empty. She licked up and down all the ridges of the scallop-shaped dish so as not to waste even one drop of this divine new flavor. When she was done, she sighed, sat back, glanced up at the king, and blinked her eyes slowly, tilting her head slightly. Would he offer her some water to help clear the thirst brought on by the salty flavor? The king must have understood, because he offered her another dish, this time of water with lemon. "Here, petit Chaton. I know that caviar makes one very thirsty. Clear your palate with some lemon water."

"Very good!" Popsy was impressed that he seemed to read her thoughts.

After a satisfying drink, she hopped down from her chair and began to give herself a bath. She licked all around each of her front toes, and then she made sure to completely moisten all across the backs of her paws in order to wipe them across her face and whiskers. Bathing was a very satisfying process; not only did it make one clean and beautiful, but sometimes it even allowed Popsy to find a lingering drop of flavor still clinging to her chin or one of her whiskers. This was like dessert, so she was always sure to be as thorough as possible.

The best part about bathing was that people had to wait for her while she did it. It was a good technique to keep humans in their place.

After her bath, Popsy stretched her legs, first reaching forward with her front paws, and then arching her back to her tiptoes. She was aware that the king was watching her, still with that quizzical smile on his face, but she no longer allowed that to bother her. They were friends now, and she didn't need to worry about his attitude. He had showed her ample respect by providing her with this wonderful meal. That's what humans were for!

Her bathing and stretching complete, Popsy decided that the time had arrived for a nap. Remembering her manners, she looked up at the king and gave two quick meows: "Thank you!" She then sauntered back into the king's bedchamber, hopped up onto his bed, curled up on the highest pillow she could find, and instantly fell into a deep sleep.

The Sun King

THE KING WAS ANNOYED. No, more than annoyed, he was angry. It had been such a beautiful day, he'd gone for a lovely ride through the countryside, and he had hoped to come home to enjoy an evening's entertainment with his favorite courtiers. But upon his return to the château, a message awaited, reminding him that yet one more contingent of Huguenots would be coming to the château tomorrow morning to request an audience with the king. With that to look forward to, he knew that he was likely to feel irritable all evening.

Louis had been troubled long enough with the trials and complaints of these Protestants. He was becoming convinced that it was time to silence them all. Certain of his councilors had tried to convince him that France would suffer if he made any changes to the state of affairs. But he was fed up with these Protestants who believed that they had "rights." He tired of this game and was ready to bring it to an end.

All of this served just to aggravate him. Louis knew that his evening might be ruined if he could not find some diversion to take his mind off of these problems. How he tired of these issues! They annoyed him like a swarm of mosquitoes at a beautiful summer picnic; however much you swatted at them, the measly bugs only seemed to increase in their intensity. At least mosquitoes would disappear after a few weeks; these Huguenots never seemed to go away!

As he sat in his apartment mulling over his political options, the doors swung open and his favorite ice artist, Edgard Le Maître de la Glace, entered carrying a magnificent sculpture. This one was of a rearing horse, and it brought welcome laughter to the king's lips and heart. It was splendid, and because of that his wife and his mistress would both be jealous of this ice sculpture! Imagine that, feeling jealousy toward a thing made of ice! It boosted Louis's sense of power, knowing that every detail of his life, even the smallest whim, had such a profound effect on those around him.

Once Edgard had poured him his first glass of champagne and bowed out of the room, Louis sat down near the glass doors to gaze at the late afternoon sun, which was close to setting. These restful moments with nobody around to pester him were rare. He was usually surrounded by many courtiers, courtesans, and servants. He always looked forward to these moments when he could drink a bit of champagne and enjoy a taste of caviar in real peace and quiet. He opened the door slightly to encourage a breath of fresh air into the room.

All of a sudden, from the corner of his eye, he caught a movement of the tablecloth that lay under the caviar and champagne. Eh? What could that be? A spy? No spy could be so small as to fit on that cart. So it surely was not a Huguenot. Louis sat quietly and watched.

He could be patient. If one of his enemies had planted something there to threaten him, he would be ready.

A few minutes went by with no more movement. Had he imagined it? Then Louis saw something poke out from behind the cloth. Aha! What was it? A weapon? A knife? He held his breath and stared. Then he realized what it was—the nose of a cat! Oh my goodness, this was quite the evening for creatures in the boudoir, was it not? First his marvelous sculpture of a rearing stallion and now this!

Louis grinned with relief and continued to observe The Nose. He could see it twitching as it sniffed the room. The only cats Louis had ever observed were the ones that lived in the royal stables—barn cats. They were good mouse chasers, but being quite wild, they always kept their distance from humans. So Louis had never been able to observe them up close. Having this creature right here in his bedchamber provided an interesting opportunity to learn something new. "A prudent creature, cautious yet brave!" he thought. Would the feline stay hidden behind the cloth, or would the remainder of the cat follow The Nose? He would just wait and see. This was certainly entertaining and exactly the kind of distraction he needed.

More minutes passed in silence. Then as the cat's curiosity drew her further out from behind the cloth, a lovely head with deep green eyes and multicolored fur parted the folds of the tablecloth. Louis was most impressed by this bold creature. She stared directly into his eyes and showed no fear!

Louis decided to address the cat. "Well, petit Chaton, who are you? What are you doing in the bedchamber of the king? Do you even know who I am? My courtiers are all afraid of me, but here you arrive, uninvited, a brazen little thing indeed!"

This seemed to enliven the creature. She hopped off the cart, strutting away from him in a most dismissive manner. Brazen indeed! Louis admired the boldness in her step. True courage was a rare quality, and he recognized it immediately in this beautiful little cat.

He chuckled as he watched her sashay away. "Here's a small diversion," Louis thought. "I'll see if I can befriend this little creature. I have heard that cats are apt to be aloof. Let me see if I can win her over. I like how daring she is!"

Glancing back at the cart he had an idea. Why not tempt her with caviar? What cat could possibly say no to that? He loved caviar himself and always had plenty on his cart. He could spare a dish for his visitor. But he didn't know if the cat would be a tidy or a messy eater, so perhaps it would be best to give this a try outside. If she escaped, it would be no great loss.

Louis stepped over to the door to his garden and opened it all the way. Taking a deep breath, he inhaled the clean air. The afternoon breeze wafted through his rosebushes, bringing their perfume his way. He breathed deeply, smiled, and turned to his visitor.

"Eh, mon petit ami, I am going to step outside to enjoy this late afternoon light. It is truly golden light, which is my favorite color. It is the color of royalty! Would you like to enjoy a little fresh air with me in the garden?"

He was pleased to see her turn, consider his proposal as if she understood every word, and then walk through the open door. Still holding her head high as she passed him in the doorway, she was the picture of grand royalty. This cat had certainly come to the right place!

Louis watched as she walked over to inspect some roses. She looked quite lovely in the late afternoon light, and he was glad that she showed no inclination to run away. She pawed around a bit in the earth, allowed herself a "personal moment", but didn't dig so deeply as to bother the plants. It seemed that she enjoyed this opportunity to be outdoors.

Walking over to a set of table and chairs, Louis seated himself and placed a dish of caviar on the chair next to him. Gently tapping the seat of the chair, he invited her to sit with him. "Come, mon petit ami, join me here at the table. I have brought you a dish of my caviar. Have you ever tasted caviar?"

The cat looked at him as he spoke. Again he had the uncanny feeling that she actually understood his words. She approached the chair and then hopped up to where he had gestured. Showing caution that was quickly overridden by curiosity, she sniffed at the caviar and took a small taste. "Ah," he thought, "this must be a new treat for her." Probably the other humans in her life would not have allowed her such an extravagant delicacy. He liked the idea that he could offer her something new and exciting. Louis enjoyed being first and best in all things, even befriending this small creature.

He watched with satisfaction as she proceeded to eat the entire plate of caviar. Who knew when the last time she had eaten was? Or what she had eaten? Clearly she was hungry now, and she finished off this meal with gusto. Even after the pearls of caviar were gone, she licked the crystal dish until it was spotless. She was a thorough little girl, wasn't she?

Suspecting that she'd now be thirsty, he offered her a dish of lemon water. She seemed most grateful for the offer, and she drank that until it too was gone. Then she hopped down off the chair.

Settling herself in the last pool of fading sunlight, she set about taking a bath. Louis had seen the royal stable cats bathe themselves, but having never had a cat inside the château before, he had never had occasion to watch this ritual up close. It was quite a production that lasted a long time, but it also seemed like a very pleasing and wonderful process. The cat did not miss even one millimeter of her paws or face. She licked and wiped her claws, paws, and face over and over until she shone. When she was finally finished washing herself, not a hair was out of place. Louis found himself wishing that the royal bathers who washed him daily would do as good a job.

Finally the cat turned, strutted back into the bedchamber, jumped up onto the royal bed, found a pillow that looked comfy, curled up into a tiny ball of elegant fluff, and fell asleep.

The Hall of Mirrors

POPSY AWOKE to find herself still on the king's pillow. All was quiet. Soft light from a few candles lit the room. She must have slept a long time; she could tell from the glow outside the glass doors that night had passed and it was early morning outside. After such a long and adventurous day, she was glad she'd been able to rest and restore herself.

Popsy was not alone. She heard the low rumble of soft snoring and realized that the shape of the king lay under the covers next to her. She must have been in a very deep sleep if he'd been able to climb into the bed without disturbing her.

She gazed about the room. Was she really here? Had she truly travelled so far from her comfortable home in Paris? Would Mamina suddenly walk in the door, pick her up, and take her home? Was this a dream or maybe just a joke of some kind? She would not be surprised if that boy, Charles, had rigged this all up as some elaborate prank. But lying here quietly next to the sleeping king, Popsy realized that this was not a dream. This was real.

As before, Popsy was very impressed at the lavish décor of this room. Obviously the king was wealthy. So, in one way, it felt appropriate that she had arrived here, since Popsy considered herself to be a feline of the highest character and breeding.

A glimmer of early morning sun was glowing just at the edge of the horizon. Nestling her head back into the curl of her front paws, Popsy decided she would watch the dawn. She could see rays of light as they began to streak across the sky, filtering through the tall oaks that lined the expanse of lawn beyond the rose garden. A reflection of light caught her eye as it arced off the surface of a lake in the distance. Not only did this king have a lovely bedchamber, but he also lived on a huge and beautiful property. This was even bigger than the lawn surrounding Mamina's country home!

Ever so slowly, the world came alive with color and sound. Popsy could hear birds beginning to chirp and sing in the garden. Sunlight lit the trees, flowers, fountains, and lawns visible through the doorway, bringing color back to the world. Bit by bit, a warm bright light began to fill the room.

Still, the king snored.

Popsy wondered if she could wake him and have some more caviar. That would make a delightful breakfast! She uncurled herself and climbed up onto the hill of his hip. She began to knead the quilt under her toes in the hope that he would feel it and awaken in a generous humor. Mamina always liked being awakened like this when she fell asleep in front of her TV.

But no, the snoring continued.

Maybe she'd need to make some noise. She tried three soft meows: "Good morning, king!"

Still, the king snored.

Well, she didn't want to make so much noise that someone else might hear. She didn't know who might be outside the bedroom door. So perhaps it was best to let him sleep some more. Maybe he had endured a long day too and needed his rest. Popsy decided that she might explore a bit until the king was awake.

Gazing around, she noticed that there was a door next to the bed that was open enough for her to peek through to the next room. There she saw walls covered with mirrors that reached up to a tall ceiling that was bursting with light. From this perspective, it looked as though this room was brighter than any other room of the king's house that she'd seen so far, more brilliant than any room she'd ever been in anywhere. Curious about what might make it so, Popsy hopped down from the bed and stuck her head through the doorway.

Brilliant light struck her and caused her to catch her breath. She stepped forward and found herself in a long room. The walls to her left were covered with tall mirrors that stretched up to the high ceilings, from which hung huge crystal chandeliers. Between the mirrors stood white marble sculptures of noble figures gazing out over the room. Facing these was a wall made entirely of glass doors, allowing a flood of morning light to fill the space. Between the doors were more sculptures; these were of young boys covered in gold leaf, each holding a crystal lamp. Above the chandeliers the ceiling was covered with elaborate paintings of military conquests. Noble and courageous figures filled the scenes.

In the center of the room, a huge golden throne with cushions covered in plush red velvet sat atop a white marble base. "How majestic!" Popsy thought. "Surely only someone of the greatest importance would be allowed to sit there. I should give it a try!"

Feeling more regal than ever before, Popsy paraded the long distance to the throne. She took her time and glanced over her shoulder to catch her image in each mirror as she strode by. She imagined rows of humans, cats, and dogs kneeling to her as she passed. How regal she appeared! At the foot of the throne, she gazed up at this seat of great authority, towering so high above her. "Alright," she coached herself, "take a deep breath. Un . . . deux . . . trois . . . allez-oop!" With one well-aimed leap, she jumped onto the seat, turned to look back over the room, and sat down with quiet dignity.

Yes, she certainly felt majestic. This was a seat made for her. From here she could look down on any human who dared to draw near.

Who is Royalty Now?

"**CHATON! QU'ES-CE QUE TU FAIS!?!**" the king screamed across the room. With all the mirrors and other hard surfaces, his voice echoed sharply back and forth around Popsy. It hurt her ears so much that she flattened them back against her head. She just hated it whenever anybody raised their voice, and this was extreme! "What are you doing? You are sitting on the royal throne! Nobody but the king is allowed to sit there! I command you to get down at once!"

Startled by the king's anger, Popsy froze and sank her claws deeper into the velvet cushion. She hunkered down closer to the seat in an attempt to disappear, or at least to shrink herself into the tiniest target she could be.

"I said *Now!*" Louis bellowed.

Popsy made herself smaller still and clung more tightly to the seat.

"Argh! Will you not obey me?" Louis roared and shook his fists as he rushed toward the throne.

Popsy sneaked a glance at the king as he ran at her, and it took all of her control not to meow in screams of cat laughter. Here was a madman, taking himself far too seriously as he ran across the room. He was wearing an ankle-length nightshirt, bright red slippers on his feet, and a silly stocking cap on his head, the point of which bounced around in front of his face. (Where had that mountain of hair gone?) He kept pushing the cap aside with the back of his hand and blowing huge puffs of exasperated breath in his attempts to clear it away. But it was all in vain; the hat would just whip around his head and hit him again from the other side. Back and forth it went, while Louis only managed to grow beet red in the face and looked quite the buffoon. How could she take him seriously? Even his nightcap disobeyed him.

Popsy breathed a sigh of relief. Her instincts told her that this was all bluster and show. He would not hurt her. So as he approached, she calmly gazed at him with her liquid green eyes. By the time he reached the throne, he was out of breath and beginning to laugh at himself. "Oh you are a brave one, Chaton! Nobody else in this kingdom would dare to defy me as you do! Well, if you will not descend from there, at least move over to make room for me. I am tired from a long night and not enough sleep. When I awoke and saw that you were gone, I was worried. Imagine that!" he chuckled, shaking his head in disbelief.

Popsy wiggled to the side and made room for Louis to join her on the throne. He hefted his derriere up onto the velvet cushion and settled in next to her, gently stroking Popsy's fur as he caught his breath. "There—this is much better now. You do make me feel calm, Chaton. If only I had been able to spend the evening with you last night instead of having to deal with my ministers. Sometimes they annoy me so."

The king continued to pet Popsy in long, pensive strokes, from the top of her head down the full length of her body to the tip of her tail, over and over. It felt very good, and she began to purr. With each repetition, he grew quieter and quieter. Only the soft sound of her purring could be heard in the room. He seemed to have fallen into a deep reverie.

Finally the king sighed and spoke again. "You know, Chaton, I have had many problems with the Protestants in my kingdom. They call themselves "Huguenots." They have always troubled me, expecting to be treated as equals to the Catholics. Are they crazy? Do they take me for a fool? Over and over they ask me for favors. I really detest them and I am fed up with the games they play. Did you know that they actually plan to approach me this morning and ask permission to build a church and open businesses in Paris? *Paris!* My city! How dare they? Of course, I will refuse. I believe that it is time for me to take action."

"Of course!" Popsy gave two assenting meows.

"Aha! You agree, do you?"

Popsy blinked twice, long and slow, looking directly into the king's eyes. He was the king, after all. All citizens should obey him (all *human* citizens, at least). Why should Louis put up with insubordination from anyone? If worshipping and doing business in Paris was an affront to the king, she didn't want them there either. After all, it was her city too!

"You know, Chaton, my grandfather Henry IV made things so difficult. Just because he used to be a Protestant before he was king, he saw fit to make a law, the Edict of Nantes, allowing all Protestants to live, worship, and do business in France. When he became a Catholic, he should have forgotten his Protestant past! Yes, he ended some wars with this edict. But that was long ago, in another century."

Popsy nodded in assent. Louis smiled as he noticed her listening and understanding him. "You are such a special cat, Chaton! If only my ministers understood me as you do!"

Louis gazed up at the ceiling and continued talking, primarily to himself, but to Popsy, too. He tapped his chin thoughtfully as he spoke. "So, I have been very tempted to revoke this Edict of Nantes. Tell me now; if I should do that, would you be in agreement with that as well? I tire of this folly. My family has saddled me with ridiculous laws."

Exasperated from the king's hesitancy, Popsy exclaimed with three sharp meows, "Just *do* it!" The path seemed very clear to her; she could not understand his indecision. Humans always made things so complicated!

"You are so right!"exclaimed the king. "What am I waiting for? I shall have my scribe begin to draw up my pronouncement today. Enough of these Protestants! I will cancel today's audience. Why should I even bother meeting with them? I am done with them all!"

Louis shifted his weight and lowered himself to the floor. Picking Popsy up in his arms, he kissed her on the top of her head and said, "This calls for a celebration! You make me so very happy, Chaton! How would you like a breakfast of more caviar? I know I would enjoy that."

Popsy purred as loudly as she could and rubbed her nose and face along his jawline to show her enthusiasm for this idea. "Finally some sensible action!" she thought.

The Sun King smiled. He felt very satisfied, as if a piece of a puzzle long out of place had finally been found and fit back where it belonged. With peace and contentment in his heart, he strode back to his bedchamber, his new best friend held tenderly in his arms.

Interlude

POPSY PROCEEDED TO LIVE a very comfortable and contented life with the king. She became Louis's primary source of relaxation. His announcement that he would revoke the Edict of Nantes caused quite an uproar in the kingdom. Some of his ministers were very pleased—they had secretly been wishing for an act like this for a long time—but many others were disturbed. They feared that an exodus of Huguenots would ensue, which could devastate the French economy. As a result, there was much debate and unrest in the château.

Louis escaped this turmoil by spending as much time with Popsy as he could. His mind was made up. No amount of clamoring between his ministers would convince him he was wrong. Popsy's quiet and sure demeanor calmed him and reinforced his confidence in his stance on this and other issues. In the life of the Sun King, problems arose every day. Louis was required be the final arbiter of most disputes that were brought before his court. With Popsy in his life, he closed the court early in the day so that he could return to his bedchamber and indulge her with some sort of delicacy. Then the two of them would wander in his gardens.

During the day, Popsy was given free rein to roam through the château. Louis made it clear to his staff that she was his Noble Pet, and as such she enjoyed a higher stature than any person in his retinue. After all, she actually slept with the king. Only his wife and mistress could make the same claim, but not on such a regular basis! The king pronounced that nobody was to harm Popsy in any way or prevent her from wandering where her curiosity led. After all, what harm could his petit chaton do to anything?

Tumbling Back

T WAS JUST BEFORE DAWN. Popsy awoke and gazed toward the window, dozing off and on in the warmth and comfort of her favorite pillow at the head of the king's bed. Finally her tummy began to rumble, and hunger brought her more fully awake. Stretching her legs, paws, and toes, she reached for the king but her toes met only an empty pillow. Where was he? Touching the king first thing in the morning had become a small ritual for Popsy. It was something that brought her back to the reality of château life, regardless of what she'd been dreaming. She patted around the pillows, searching for him in the darkness to no avail. Ah, yes! She stopped and shook her head. Now she remembered that the king had told her he'd be gone for the weekend. Off to meet with some council in a faraway city.

She was on her own for a few days.

In her slumber, she had enjoyed visions of Mamina. These were sweet dreams filled with images of the apartment in Paris. Her bed by the window; the courtyard below; Mamina and her dear family; even that human boy, Charles—all these thoughts brought to her mind faces that spoke of comfort and safety and . . . home. Home? Really? Where *was* her home anymore?

Certainly she was very happy and comfortable here with the king. She loved receiving royal treatment, eating caviar and other delicacies, and having her way in all things. Life could not be better. But somewhere in the back of her mind, she felt an emptiness. She missed the sweet sing-song voice Mamina used as she chatted with her in the kitchen. She missed "Popsy plage," the make-believe little beach that Mamina would set up for her next to the kitchen sink. Mamina's apartment and lifestyle were not as extravagant as the king's, but there was a certain "je ne sais quoi" in their relationship that she longed for.

Popsy hopped down from the bed and walked over to get a sip of water from the dish that was kept for her by the windows. She gazed at her own reflection in the dark windowpane and pondered, "What shall I do today? Hm. I'm on my own. Maybe I'll explore new corners of the château!" A small pang reminded her again of hunger, so she decided to go to the kitchen to see what morsels the chef had for her. He was a generous man and always saved her pieces of liver, fish, and other tasty snacks.

She trotted out of the bedchamber giving a quick "meow" in greeting to the attendants who stood guard. They nodded their heads in acknowledgment of her, but she could hear whispered comments behind her back as she moved through the antechamber. She often had the feeling that they resented her. She waved goodbye to them by giving a sharp swish of her tail as she walked on.

Moving forward from salon to hallway to staircase, from room to room, she worked her way toward the kitchen—the nerve center of the château, in her opinion! She knew the way well, and meowed a little tune to herself as she trotted along.

In the middle of one staircase, she noticed an open window. This was odd, it had always been closed before. The window faced an alley where carts and horses passed by, day in and day out. Popsy jumped up on the sill to get a better look and breathe in the fresh air. The soft light of the chandelier behind her shone out upon the grass below. She could see her own shadow on the ground; she straightened up to make herself more regal than she already was. It was a cold and grey dawn, but the fresh air still smelled much better than the stale air in the closed-up rooms of the château. For some reason that Popsy could not understand, the inhabitants of this château seemed almost fearful of clean air. Doors and windows were most often closed, making rooms stifled and hot. The smell of burnt wax from all the candles hung heavy in the air. Warmth was a good thing, to be sure, but fresh air was divine!

Popsy leaned out the window to peek at the ground below in the hopes that there might be a garden or fountain or fish pond she could explore. But no, the street came so close to the walls of the château that there was no room for much except a strip of grass. But even fresh grass smelled good on a wet day like this. Popsy took a deep breath, savoring the rich aroma of the moist earth below.

Suddenly she spied a faint movement out of the corner of her eye. What could that be? A mouse? Some small creature she could hunt and pounce on? She twisted on the windowsill to catch a better view, but in the effort, she spun too far. She slipped, her hind legs shooting out from under her. She ended up dangling precariously from the sill, clinging with her front claws and frantically kicking her hind legs. She tried to get a hold underneath to keep from slipping all the way out, but to no avail. Her hind feet could find no crevice in the wall, nothing to catch onto or push against. Her back claws scratched the wall in vain. In an attempt to gain a better hold with her front paws, she tried to reach further into the window, but that split second of release proved a mistake. She lost control completely and fell to the ground below.

It was only about a ten foot drop. Like all cats do when they fall, Popsy let her natural balancing skills take over as she fell, and her body twisted to right itself. She landed on all four feet, unhurt. She gave herself a good shake, and then crouched down in an instinctive move to hide. Recalling the breathing techniques she had used that first day of her arrival, she took a moment to regain her composure. Then, feeling ready to jump back up to the window, she turned and looked up. Mon Dieu! The window was closed! No light shone from the hallway inside. No sign of life stirred. It just looked like an old window set in an ancient wall that no human had touched in centuries.

Despondent and confused, Popsy turned to face the road again. Suddenly a whoosh of water splashed over her as she heard a loud "honk". What? A car? What happened to the carts and horses? How did cars suddenly reappear in the world?

Soaked to the skin and quivering in fear, Popsy froze in place, afraid to make another move. Again she caught a slight movement out of the corner of her eye, just as she had seen from the window. With a racing heart, she turned oh-so-slightly to look and see what was there. She gasped, finding herself face-to-face with a creature unlike any she had ever seen before. The animal was long and slender, its tail equal in length to its body. Its color was a tawny brown except for a dark grey mask that covered the upper part of its face and eyes like that character she had seen on Mamina's television—Zorro. It had coal-black eyes and rounded little ears that stuck straight up, making it look very alert. Its masked face was so close she could feel its warm breath on her check. It stared intently into her eyes. It blinked. It moved a little closer. Then it asked in a soft voice, "Are you lost too?"

Francois

"AND PLEASE, MON FILS, be very careful not to get lost. Try to stay only near the main avenue. And of course, do your best to come back with something for us to eat!" Francois's mother gave him a hug and a peck on the cheek as he crawled out of their burrow. As the oldest weasel kit in the family, Francois felt responsible to help find food for his mother and the babies in their nest. It seemed that the little ones never stopped crying for something to eat. His mother, Claudine, could not hunt every hour of the day and care for them too. So his help was essential to their survival.

What a winter this had been! In late December a raging windstorm had slammed through Versailles. All the oldest trees in the parks and in town had toppled over, exposing their ancient roots to the wintry sky. In those root systems had lived dozens of families of ground-dwelling creatures, mostly weasels, including Francois' family. Suddenly homeless after the storm, weasels and other creatures had wandered the streets for weeks, looking for shelter from the weather and any food they could steal along the way.

Francois would never forget the horrible night his family's nest had been exposed. Howling winds had whipped at the trunk and branches of the tree under which his family had lived. Wood had creaked and groaned around him, sounding like tortured ghosts shrieking in the night. Mingled with the frightened cries of his baby brothers and sisters, he had feared these sounds would drive him mad. But through it all, Francois had done his best to be brave. He had to act like an adult weasel so that he could help his mother protect the babies.

With a tremendous ripping noise, their home tree had begun to fall. Creaking and groaning, the top of the tree had slowly tipped over, more and more, as the roots of the tree lifted their nest into the violent night air. With one final crash, the tree had slammed to the ground, completely uprooted.

Rain and wind had pelted the weasel family as they wriggled out of the nest that was now held high in the air along with the exposed roots. They had dropped to the ground and run for their lives. They had dashed blindly at first, in wild zigzags, driven by their panic to get away from the falling tree limbs. Once away from their home tree, they had still had to run from other falling trees. It had seemed that the whole world was crashing down around them.

Eventually they had found a little bit of shelter under a large board that had blown off of a neighboring roof and become lodged between a parked car and a stone wall. They had huddled together under this board through the night, keeping each other warm.

Francois and his family had roamed for a week or more, scavenging food as best they could and searching for a new home. A couple of times they had thought they'd found a likely nook or burrow, only to discover that another weasel family had claimed the spot already. These encounters had always included much hissing, spitting, baring of sharp little teeth, and arched backs as the two families faced off.

Claudine had maintained that she had no interest in making another weasel family homeless, so they had always slowly backed away from these confrontations to turn and continue on their search. It was a long hard journey. Just when it felt as though they'd never find a new home, they discovered a hole leading into the ground next to an old fence post. Francois had crawled down and found a cave-like nesting space that would suit the family very well. Dry, protected, and somewhat removed from the center of town, it was pleasantly quiet. Claudine had hoped that she and Francois could hunt in the nearby fields for voles and mice to sustain them. For many weeks, the hunting had been good. They'd been able to eat well, and the babies had cried less often. But in the past few days, neither Claudine nor Francois had been able to catch anything at all.

So, this morning, Claudine advised Francois that he should cautiously explore the streets in town closer to the château to see if any garbage bins were open and accessible. Trash was not her preferred diet, but her babies were starving, and rejected food was better than none at all.

So Francois set out to explore the town. He'd been through here before, but never alone, and he felt very grown up to be out on his own on the streets like this. He scampered along the sidewalk, ducking under parked cars at every opportunity. He followed the main avenue, and at each crossing he looked to see if it was a back alley or if there was any refuse set out on the side of the street. He came across one bin and leapt up to peek inside. Clinging to the top, he nudged the lid aside with his nose. Inside he could see that there was only paper in this container. No smell of anything edible reached his nose, so he dropped to the ground and continued his search.

He did his best to keep out of sight. His mother had warned him that humans didn't like weasels, and he could be in grave danger if he got spotted. Humans would certainly chase him away and might even try to kill him. So he sprinted in short little bursts from car to bench to stone wall and back, trying to keep hidden as best he could.

One bin next to a bench smelled as if it might have some food in it. He hopped onto the bench, stood on his hind legs, and stuck his nose inside. Yes! There, right on top of the other refuse, was a small crust of bread with a hint of cheese clinging to it. Ravenous with hunger, Francois gobbled this down. He would keep looking for something to take home to his family, but this little bit would keep him going for a longer search.

With his head buried in the bin, he suddenly heard a screech so close that he felt as though his little ears would burst. "Ai! A weasel! Right there on the bench! Take *that*, you filthy rodent! Va t'en!" There was an explosion of sound as an umbrella smacked down on the bench right next to Francois, just missing him by a hair. Francois leapt off the bench and ran as fast as he could to escape this attack. Terrified, he paid no attention to his direction, running blindly to save himself.

His heart beat in a wild staccato rhythm, and he gasped for breath as he ran. In his determination to flee his attacker, he even ran wildly across one of the wide main streets, his terror increasing as cars zoomed every which way around him. Finally he slowed and huddled, panting, next to the base of some old masonry. He was at the château now. He recognized it, but was unsure how he'd gotten here. He closed his eyes. He curled into a tiny ball. He tucked his nose under his tail. He took one huge, deep breath, then another, and another, until finally he felt the panic ebb away, and he rested for a minute or two.

Opening his eyes again, he looked around trying to find something familiar. Any landmark would do: a wall, a gate, a bench, anything that would help him figure out what direction he'd come from and where he'd need to go to return home. His heart sank as he realized that it all looked foreign. He closed his eyes, trying to let his wild weasel senses take over. "Home, home, where is home? Do I feel the pull? Do I feel a draw?" Nothing. At least he did know that he was at the château. If worst came to worst, he'd have to circle it until he saw a street that he recognized.

Suddenly he heard a window open above him. Glancing up, he gasped. There, poised on the windowsill, he saw a vision that took all his worries away. Gazing out over the street was the most beautiful creature he'd even seen. "Oh, mon Dieu!" he whispered to himself. She was exquisite! She looked to be about as long as he was but not so slender and slinky. She had a fuller body, covered with long, luxurious fur of white, gold, and black. Her eyes were a pure green and shone out from beneath her brow in a contented manner as she scanned the neighborhood. His heart quickened a beat again, but not from panic this time. It was adoration he felt.

He shifted his position to gain a better look, and as he did so, he could tell that she saw his movement. She attempted to turn her body on the sill—perhaps to return his gaze? But—ah non! She slipped! He saw her scramble in a frenzied effort to regain her hold on the sill, but to no avail. She fell to the ground, landing neatly on her feet. How did she do that? How did she land so expertly?

As Francois gazed at her in admiration, a car whizzed by, hitting a puddle which sent a wave of muddy water over this creature. He could see that she was suddenly soaked to the skin. "Poor thing," he thought. "One shock to her system after another!'

He crept closer, until she was inches away from his face. He could see panic in her eyes. Francois kept still and quiet, not wanting to startle her more. He watched as she regained her composure, and then he saw her turn, readying herself for a high jump back to the windowsill. As she glanced up to gauge the distance for her leap, he followed her gaze and saw that the window had been closed. There would be no easy return for her!

With quiet caution, he crept nearer to this creature. She turned. He caught her gaze. Exquisite, she was absolutely exquisite. He took a breath. Then he asked, "Are you lost, too?"

New Friends

WHAT A STRANGE CREATURE Popsy found in front of her—she'd never seen anything quite like him. So slender and sleek, with a long tail, sharp claws poking out between furry toes on all four feet, pointed little teeth that glistened as he spoke, and that mask! The mask made him look like he had something to hide. He seemed like a creature built for speed and aggression. And yet his approach to her seemed friendly, not hostile or threatening. How should she respond? Tell the truth? Feign indifference?

She intuitively felt that she could use a friend. Somehow her instincts told her that the king could not help or protect her anymore. There were cars, modern automobiles whizzing past on the road. The smell of exhaust assaulted her senses for the first time in weeks. No horses or carts were visible anywhere. And across the street, she saw someone walking in clothing similar to Mamina's. She could feel that there had been a shift, some drastic change to this world she'd inhabited since her arrival in the seafood truck. She felt as though she had just tumbled through a long tunnel and come out . . . where?

She had to admit that an ally might be very helpful just now.

Drenched from the water that had splashed over her, Popsy began to feel a chill. Shivering from cold and worry, she said in a shaky voice, "Yes, I am a bit lost. And cold."

The creature spoke again. "Let me see if I can help you lose that chill. It's because you are all wet. Here, move away from the street. Oh, and my name is Francois. Enchanté!" He closed his eyes for a moment and bowed his head before her.

With gentle nudges, Francois coaxed Popsy to move away from the street and the puddles. Then he began to lick her coat in long, slow movements. Starting at her cheeks and nose, then between her ears, down her neck and back, across her sides, and finishing with a flourish on her tail, he used his tongue to remove all the excess water that had been splashed over her. With each little lick, Popsy felt a flicker of warmth. The rhythm of this cleansing massage was so peaceful and tender she was almost lulled into a trance. By the time Francois was done, she felt very comforted and quite warm again.

Popsy turned her head to look at him and blinked with contentment. "Thank you so much. You are very good at that! How did you know to care for me so well? Oh, and my name is Popsy," she said, bobbing a small curtsy back at him.

"Well, I have many little brothers and sisters. They get themselves into all kinds of trouble. My mother, Claudine, taught me that trick long ago. It keeps them from crying when they are cold, calms their fears, and helps them to stay healthier too."

A family! He had a family! Popsy sighed. She longed for her family now. Oh, to be someplace familiar and safe! To feel the comfort of daily noises, smells, and routines. She would give anything to be home again.

"I came here looking for food to feed my brothers and sisters. But I was chased by a human, and in a moment of panic, I ran away and have lost all sense of direction. I need to continue on; I must find some food, and I must find my way home. I would really like your company. Would you join me?"

Popsy nodded. She would put her trust in him.

They looked around, trying to get some sense of their bearings. Having originally arrived here in the total blackness of the shrimp truck, Popsy had no visual memory of the streets or the buildings. She had never seen them before. But just as a cat can fall from a great height and flip over to land neatly on four paws, so too could Popsy get a sense of where they needed to go. It was as if a magnetic pull was gently tugging at her, telling her to circle around the château. "I think I know. Follow me," she said.

Taking the lead, Popsy moved in cautious little steps, keeping low and quiet against the wall of the château. Francois followed her, staying so close she could feel his warm breath on her back.

Following the château wall, slinking, stopping, hiding, and darting their way, they arrived at a large bustling intersection. Popsy's senses told her that they would need to cross this huge avenue. Somehow she knew they should move away from the château and head for the homes that lined the city street that stretched off into the distance. But with so many trucks and cars zooming past, it seemed an impossible feat to make that crossing.

She and Francois discussed the possibilities. They watched as traffic surged back and forth, cars and trucks crisscrossing each other in an unending stream of movement and noise. The air was filled with a cacophony of horns honking, tires squealing, and engines revving. They observed the traffic carefully, trying to see if there was any pattern to the movement, any way to predict an opening through which they could dash. It seemed impossible.

But after a few more minutes, Francois pointed to a post with lights on it. He told Popsy to watch as the lights changed color. First one would brighten and then another—never two at a time. Occasionally one or two humans would cross the street. Francois and Popsy watched to see if they could discern a pattern. Finally Francois pointed out to her that the people only walked across the road when the uppermost light was lit.

"That is it," whispered Popsy. "We have to wait for that top light and then rush across! Francois, you are so smart!"

Francois smiled, feeling quite proud, but stayed quiet. He still needed to refine this idea. Crossing this street would be a life-or-death moment. Popsy was glad to see that he took this decision so seriously.

After five or six more repetitions of the lights changing, feeling sure that they'd identified just the right moment, Francois placed a paw on Popsy's shoulder and said, "Let's go on the next turn of the light. See, there is a whole group of humans who will be crossing too. Maybe we can run in between their feet and be protected from being hit that way."

Popsy nodded her head. She was ready, but her heart was pounding with anxiety about this risky maneuver. Once again she relied on her breathing technique to calm herself and focus.

Francois, his eyes riveted on the lights, said to her softly, "Alright now, Popsy. I will count. Get ready! On three. Un . . . deux . . . trois . . . allons-y! Vite!"

They dashed out into the middle of the group of humans who were beginning to cross the avenue. Shoes crashed to the right and the left, falling like huge boulders all around them. But they stayed in the center of the group, praying that they could make the crossing without getting crushed. Popsy's tail got stepped on, and Francois received a small kick in the side, but they did not stop to whine or worry about these minor injuries. They must get across now!

And then, just as suddenly as they'd begun, they reached the other curb. They scurried away from the humans and huddled over at the base of the nearest building. Heaving a big sigh of relief, Popsy exclaimed, "We did it! We are safely across!"

Close by, they saw a low wall with an iron grid fence above it. To get away from the street, they hopped over the wall and huddled down in the shadows. Popsy could smell horses here. She could hear the clip-clop of their feet on the cobblestones. Looking around, she saw no old carriages; cars were parked in this courtyard. But horses were visible, too. From time to time, large, statuesque white horses were led across the yard from one door to another. Popsy guessed this was the château stables. The smell of the horses was comforting to her.

Once their nerves had settled a bit, Francois and Popsy talked about their options. They decided that it would be better stay right where they were for the remainder of the day. It was unsettling to be around so many humans, and they both agreed that they'd rather look for food at night.

Francois suggested that they take turns napping, and Popsy agreed. She offered to stay awake to stand guard. So Francois curled up into a tiny ball of fur at her feet, looked up into her eyes, blinked two times, gave a tiny yawn, and then shut his eyes, falling into a deep slumber. Popsy marveled at how such a long creature could fold into such a small package. The beautiful coloring of his coat glistened even in the shadows as his sides rose and fell quietly with his breathing. Popsy sat next to him, listening to each passerby on the other side of the wall. She nestled against the wall and proudly guarded her new friend as he slept.

The Search

I**T WAS DARK NOW.** Versailles was quieter. A few cars drove by from time to time, and not all of the humans were off the streets, but it was definitely quieter. There was moonlight, which allowed Popsy and Francois to see the buildings and cars and trees around them. Still hiding behind the wall in this cobbled courtyard, they heard only an occasional human or two walk by.

During their rest, Popsy told Francois all about home, about Mamina, the apartment, the courtyard. She explained about the seafood truck and the king. She ended her story saying, "Now? I just wish to be home again. I would love to be curled up beside Mamina as she reads a book or as she watches TV. I do not wish to live on the street."

Francois told Popsy about the terrible storm that had caused the loss of his home. She shuddered to think of the nightmare that he and his family had endured. No wonder he was so devoted to his mother and his siblings. They'd been through so much together!

Both Francois and Popsy were hungry. They needed to go in search of food. Not only did they need to feed themselves, Francois also needed to find something he could carry home to his family. They stood up on their tiptoes, side by side, peering over the low wall. The coast seemed clear. It was time.

With a quick pop-pat, they hopped over the wall onto the sidewalk and trotted off toward the avenue that led away from the château. Crossing the side streets was easy now. There were some cars, but not as many as during the day; it was easy to see them coming in the distance, and Popsy and Francois felt confident running in between them. There was not even a need to watch those lights before deciding to go each time.

If she hadn't been so hungry, Popsy would have enjoyed this freedom. She'd never been outside at night before. The king, like Mamina, always insisted that she be indoors before nightfall. So this sense of liberation in the dark was a new thrill for her. It made her feel secretive and special.

Popsy and Francois had fallen into an easy and comfortable friendship. Hiding out together during the day, sharing their life stories, and making decisions about their survival had forged a bond of trust. Popsy really preferred to have a friend, a companion, rather than to go it alone through the day. She found it very comforting. As she thought more about it, she realized she'd always had someone close, even in those times when she pretended that she didn't care. Mamina was her best friend ever; the king had been a fun and exciting playmate and had spoiled her endlessly; and now Francois had become her partner in . . . what? Survival? Despite her sometimes aloof demeanor, Popsy really liked knowing that she had at least one close companion she could rely on. She was very grateful that Francois had been right there when she fell from the window.

Walking down the avenue, they took a good look into the shadows of each side street as they passed. Lifting their noses, they sniffed for any promising scents. Was there anything there they could grab? Any leftovers to quell the grumbling in their tummies? This town of Versailles was clean and tidy, making it a wonderful place for humans to live but a tough place for creatures of the night to scavenge.

They walked for a long time. It felt like hours. They wandered further and further away from the château, encountering no scent of food. Driven by thirst as much as hunger, they would eagerly lap up any little bit of water that they passed. Drain spouts that had trickled a few drops of water into small depressions in the ground offered occasional sips, which they shared. But it was never enough to quench their thirst.

Occasionally, as they crossed a street, Francois would hesitate, unsure if they should cross or not. At those moments, he looked to Popsy. She would sit for a moment, close her eyes and let her senses take over. Where were they headed? She didn't really know, but each time she would experience a strong pull in one direction or another. Then she'd open her eyes and tell Francois, "I think we must go *this* way. Let's give it a try." In this manner, they progressed further and further along in a zigzag fashion, combing all the streets and alleys in their search.

Eventually Popsy began to despair. This town was just so tidy! Would they never find anything to eat? Her legs grew tired and her paws ached from walking along so much pavement, cement, and cobblestones. This was the longest distance she'd ever walked, and she was beginning to feel lightheaded. But she didn't complain. Each moment that she felt even the littlest bit scared or sorry for herself, she would remind herself of the struggles that Francois and his family had endured during that terrible storm. If his family could survive that nightmare, she could bear this a little longer.

Claudine

THREE DAYS HAD PASSED since Francois had left their den. The children had fussed a lot, mostly at night. The poor dears were so tired and hungry. Finally they had curled up into a heap of fur and whiskers and fallen asleep, too tired to even cry any more. Claudine sat watching over them, grateful to have a little bit of peace and quiet. She loved to watch her kits as they slept. It was so relaxing to watch their little breaths, their sides rising and falling almost in unison. Just an occasional wiggle of a nose or twitch of a whisker would identify one child or another in the tangled hill of fur.

She had grown very fond of this new home. It had a rich deep smell of earth, and it was divinely quiet. Their last den, over in the château park, was surrounded by many other weasel homes. Over the centuries, many dens had been dug under those ancient trees. There had been comfort in the proximity of so many weasel families, but some of the others were noisy, and their raucous behavior often broke the lovely silences. This privacy felt like a real blessing.

She was very worried about Francois. He was such a good boy, and she knew that he would take this mission of finding food very seriously. But he was a terrible navigator. Sometimes she'd swear he could get lost right here in their den. Now that he'd been gone for so long, she worried that he'd gone astray or come to some harm. She'd not be able to rest until he was home safe and sound.

The weather had been kind at first, but tonight it had begun to rain, and it still had not stopped. Claudine was now concerned that Francois was not only lost but cold and hungry too.

She heaved a sigh and realized that she would have to go looking for him. She just could not bear to wait any longer. But then who would look over the little ones? It would have to be Mathilde, the next oldest kit. Yes, Mathilde was the one she could count on; Mathilde was quiet and sensible, the most reliable of the kits.

Claudine bowed her head, closed her eyes, and whispered a little prayer to the Weasel Goddess, asking her to look over Francois until Claudine could find him and bring him safely back to their den. A warmth spread over her shoulders as she prayed, giving her a sense of peace and hope. It was almost as if the Weasel Goddess had reached down and touched her gently.

Claudine climbed up to the mouth of the hole that led down to their den. She had been going outside to check for any sign of Francois almost every fifteen minutes throughout the evening. Each time, she had emerged expectantly from their burrow, searching and sniffing for signs of her son. Then, disappointed and anxious, she had returned to her brood below.

Now she looked over the grass of the field where they lived, squinting in her effort to see some sign of Francois through the grey drizzle of the incessant rain. She lifted her nose and sniffed to see if she could detect any scent of him. All she could smell was moist dirt and grass. Ever since the storm this winter, that smell always gave her a sense of dread.

Claudine took another deep breath, hoping for some trace of her son's scent, but she found not even a hint. She sighed, waited a minute, and tried again—still no familiar odor or sign. This was enough; she could wait no longer. Too much time had passed, and she needed to go find Francois. With a quick little bark, she called Mathilde to the entrance of the den.

"My dear, I am going into town to find your brother. I fear he has gotten lost or fallen into some kind of serious trouble. There are so many dangers in town—cars, people, and . . ." Claudine could not even bring herself to say the word "dogs." She shuddered at the mere thought of Francois being chased or cornered by a dog. The image was more than she could bear. "You must stand guard here. Do not let any of the babies out alone. I hope I will not be gone too long. Pray that when you see me again, your brother will be with me and we will have some food. I'm off!"

Mathilde nodded seriously. She could tell that her mother was deeply concerned about her dear brother, and she wanted to do anything she could to help. "Oui, Maman. I will watch the others carefully. I will only bring them up one by one to have a drink of this fresh rain from the sipping pool we dug."

Claudine hugged her daughter, her sweet child, and with that, she darted away from the den toward town.

A Reunion of Weasels

FRANCOIS AND POPSY lay together, huddled in a
hole they'd discovered in a wall. A rainstorm had begun,
and they'd been pelted by the large heavy drops for an hour
or more until they had located this spot. It provided shelter to keep
the driving rain from hitting them directly, but they still got wet from
the drops splashing outside of the hole.

Before long they were both soaked to the skin and very muddy. In
their effort to find food, they'd been splashed by cars that drove through
filthy puddles. Popsy was tempted to simply go stand in the rain to get
clean, but Francois cautioned her that she might become dangerously cold.
So instead they wrapped their bodies together, shivering in this niche that
at the least kept them out of the wind. Francois tried to clean Popsy as he
had when they first met, but no sooner had he licked some part of her dry
than she would get soaked again. It was not really worth the effort.

They had actually found a little bit of food the previous evening,
a slice of quiche and a small piece of fish wrapped in newspaper that

must have been dropped from someone's market basket. What a find! It took all their restraint not to gobble down every bite. But they were both determined that Francois would eventually take the food home to his family. So instead they nibbled just a bit to quiet their hunger and then dragged the items along as they wandered the streets, looking for a way for them to get him home.

Snuggling even closer together in their hiding place, they fell into a fitful slumber, each comforted by the rhythm of the other's breathing and the warmth of their embrace. With soft little snuffles, they both dreamed of sun and warmth and family, alternated by night-mare visions of being chased by dogs and humans.

Suddenly they both awoke with a start. They heard a voice whis-pering, "Where *is* he? Here? No. Oh dear, oh dear, where could he be? Over there? Ah, yes, oh my goodness, *yes!*" A noise nearby told them that someone was approaching. They could hear panting and quick little footsteps. Now that someone was standing right outside the hole! Popsy felt a nose sniffing her all over, from head to toe. They'd been found out! Oh no! They'd been seen—but by whom?

"Mon petit Francois! How cold and wet you are! Who is this creature wrapped around you? How did you come to make friends with . . . a *cat*? Oh, mon Dieu! What are you thinking? Quick, get away with me!"

Francois burst out of the hole and leapt up, dancing, laughing, tumbling and screaming with delight. "Maman! C'est TOI! Don't worry, this is my friend, and it is alright. I am so happy to see you! I was lost—but I do have some food and this is my friend—her name is Popsy and she fell from the château window almost right on top of me and we became friends and she found the quiche and I found the fish and Popsy is helping me stay warm and we traveled together all over this town to find food and I really, really hope you like her!"

Suddenly Claudine and Francois burst into wild and joyous celebration. They wound their long sinuous bodies into a huge swarming knot as they chattered, whistled, and sang their thrill of being together again. Popsy could not help laughing out loud as she watched mother and son rejoicing. What a reunion! They climbed all over each other, practically tying their lithe bodies in knots as they simultaneously hugged and jumped with delight. All Popsy could see was a blur of fur in motion. Finally they fell apart, panting and laughing as they caught their breath. Popsy loved this; it was pure happiness, and it felt very good.

Having caught her breath, Claudine gave a long sigh and turned to face Popsy. Tilting her head to one side, she took a moment to look Popsy over carefully, nodding and whispering, "Yes, oh yes, a beautiful creature. Very polite and patient too." With great care she extended one toe from a front paw and traced the line of Popsy's chin, and then gently patted her on the shoulder.

"Thank you, my dear, for befriending my son and helping him find this food. My name is Claudine. Popsy is your name? Given to you by some human who loves you, I expect. How gracious and thoughtful you are to have saved such large portions of this feast for my children. You must be hungry and thirsty, and yet you held aside this nourishment for little creatures that you have not even met. I think you have an exquisite character. Such generosity is uncommon. Most other animals would have gorged themselves just to satisfy their own cravings without giving thought to anyone else."

Blushing, Popsy found herself tongue-tied. It was not often that she had nothing to say, but Claudine's effusive statements caught her off guard, surprising and pleasing her. It had not occurred to her to eat all this food. Of course she wanted Francois's family to have it!

"Do you live here in the streets of Versailles?" Claudine asked, holding Popsy in a steady gaze.

"Oh no, Madame. I live in Paris. In the fifteenth arrondissement with Mamina. She takes excellent care of me. She brushes me with great care, and when I am good, she gives me shrimp! Sometimes she arranges towels next to the kitchen sink to make "Popsy Plage" so that we can pretend we are at the beach. But that was before, during a time that seems long ago. Now I don't know how to get back." Popsy shook her head slowly. The reality of being so lost dawned on her even more as she spoke the words.

Placing a gentle arm around Popsy's shoulders, Claudine asked, "How did you end up here, so far from home, my dear?"

Popsy began to recount the events of that fateful day weeks ago. Suddenly the whole story spilled out of her in a furious torrent of words. "One morning some weeks ago, I went into the courtyard to perform my daily inspection and was tempted by the smell of shrimp in a fish truck and got caught in the dark and was taken away on a long drive and when we stopped there were horses and carts and then I chased a mouse and ended up in a long-ago castle and I hid on a table roulante but was discovered by the king who became my friend and he fed me caviar which is just the best seafood you ever tried and we lived together and made important political decisions together and I slept on high pillows and everyone had to be nice to me but then one day I fell from a window and by the time I hit the ground years had flown by and I was splashed by a car and suddenly there was your son and we made friends and rested together and hunted for food together and kept each other warm. And now . . . you are here." She stopped and took a deep breath. Then, with sadness in her voice, she looked back and forth from Claudine to Francois and said, "Now Francois will go home with you, and he should, but I will be left alone because I have nowhere to go, and I really do miss Mamina."

Claudine patted Popsy and gave her a tender lick on the cheek—a weasel kiss. "My dear, I would not dream of leaving you alone here on the street. You are a friend of the family now, and we must help you find your way back to your Mamina. Let me think. What to do, what to do." Claudine sat back on her haunches, chin in paw, and her fingers drummed a light rhythm against her cheek. Suddenly her eyes brightened. She sat upright, murmuring to herself, "Hmm . . . well, yes . . . ah, maybe . . . not sure . . . a little risky, but it's worth a try!"

Claudine turned, looked directly into Popsy's eyes and placed her front paws onto Popsy's shoulders. "Here is what I think, my dear. As I was combing the streets for my son, I noticed another cat who looked a bit like you. Not as beautiful, of course, but I would guess the same age and size as you. I have seen this cat on previous visits. She always looks very well-fed and groomed, as though she is pampered by some human, much as your Mamina cares for you. When I saw her tonight, she was rushing through the rain. I saw her turn the corner of that building over there, run to that side door, and suddenly she was gone! Like magic, she completely disappeared! Of course, I don't believe in magic unless the Weasel Goddess is involved, so I'll bet there is some special cat entrance to that home. I think you should go there too. Certainly a human lives there who knows how to care for a cat, and that is the kind of help you need."

Popsy looked across the street to the house that Claudine had indicated. A warm light shone through the windows of the lower floors; a few seconds went by and then Popsy saw the shadow of a person pass by one of those windows. Popsy imagined a woman, like Mamina, opening a can of cat food, spooning it onto a plate, and placing it on the floor next to a bowl of clean water for her kitty. Something tugged at her heart, a feeling that this place would feel safe and familiar. She wanted someone to give her a bowl of fresh water, too.

But then she thought about walking through the drenching rain and wind. Would she be able to find the magic doorway? What would she say to the other cat? "Hello, I'm here to eat your food"? Would there be a fight? What would *she* do if a cat just wandered into Mamina's apartment? She would protect her home! What if the other cat began to hiss and spit? Would the woman intervene? So many unknowns— this could be a step into a nest of peril. But if she didn't at least look inside, she would never know.

Claudine placed a paw under Popsy's chin. "I won't send you off alone. Francois and I will walk with you to find the door. We will be with you right up until the last step. But you must go. You must give this a try. Do not be afraid, but pay attention and be aware."

Popsy rose and turned to face the street. She trembled with anxiety, but she knew that Claudine was right. Reminding herself of her relaxation exercise, she took a deep breath and exhaled, then another deep breath, followed again by a slow and careful exhale. Another minute of this helped her to quiet her heart and steady her nerves. Francois moved over to stand at her left side; Claudine waited patiently on her right. Popsy looked at each of them, giving them a nod and the bravest smile she could muster.

Together, they stepped off the curb and walked toward the house.

Madame Testoubay

MADAME TESTOUBAY had just set down a meal for her kitty, Melki, and turned to go back to the kitchen to make her own dinner. She suddenly heard a deep growling, followed by hissing and spitting. She spun around to see Melki with her back arched and every hair on her body standing on end, her usual sleek frame puffed up to twice its real size.

Facing Melki was a measly looking little creature standing close to the food dish, shivering from cold and soaked from the rain. Despite her miserable appearance and tiny size, she was a courageous little thing who stood her ground with no fear in her eyes. She stared straight back at Melki, a low rumbling growl coming from her throat too. Fortunately, no scratches or bites had been dealt yet; there was just a lot of posturing and threatening.

Being well-accustomed to handling animals of many species, Madame Testoubay knew that she must separate these two immediately. She snatched up her own kitty and closed her safely in the next room. Turning back to look down on the half-starved, rain-drenched, and mud-spattered creature at her feet, she was unsure whether this was a cat at all. My goodness, what if Melki had been bitten? What terrible disease might she have caught? Many weasels were running around Versailles this spring due to all the uprooted trees; could this be one? Would a weasel even come through a cat door? Well, perhaps if it was hungry enough.

The cat returned her gaze, looking directly into her eyes. Then the poor creature heaved a deep sigh, gave two small meows and tilted her head to one side slowly blinking her long-lashed eyes. Madame Testoubay realized then that this was indeed a cat—a lovely one and a lost one—but what to do? She hated the thought of tossing the animal out into the cold and rain. That would be just too cruel and unfeeling. Well, first she'd let the poor thing eat and drink.

Madame Testoubay regarded the creature as she wolfed down the meal meant for Melki. The poor thing was starving! With a sigh, she decided that the cat could spend one night here. She'd keep the cats in separate rooms; no need to upset Melki any more. Then Madame Testoubay could take this cat to her veterinarian, Dr. Jerome, in the morning. He would be able to examine the kitty, and if they were lucky, they would find a tattoo, a microchip, or some other identifying mark. She knew that Dr. Jerome had equipment for reading microchips. Perhaps this cat would be listed on a database. It would be wonderful if she could actually help reunite the animal with her owner! It would certainly be worth a try.

She walked back to the kitchen to make an extra bowl of dinner for Melki. She knew it would be best to keep the cats separate. Once the intruder was done with her dinner, Madame Testoubay would try to towel her off and clean her up a bit.

After giving Melki her dinner, a fresh bowl of water, and an extra little piece of filet from her own dinner as a special treat, Madame Testoubay returned to check on their guest. The little cat had finished eating and drinking all of her food and water and had begun to groom herself. With long methodical licks of her tongue, the kitty wiped each section of her body clean. It took quite a while but was mesmerizing to watch. Madame decided not to interfere. It would probably calm the cat down, and she didn't want to risk getting scratched or bitten herself. In the morning, she'd get her cat carrier, put a dish of food in it to tempt the kitty, and take her to Dr. Jerome.

Madame Testoubay gathered some towels from her closet and arranged them into a comfy bed for the cat. She smiled to see the kitty walk over and make herself at home right away. Popsy stood on the pile of towels, kneading back and forth and up and down with her front claws. A soft purring came from her throat and she closed her eyes in feline ecstasy. She lay down and curled up into a tight little ball on top of the towels. She closed her eyes and fell fast asleep.

Mamina

MAMINA GAVE HER NAME at the reception desk and took a seat in the waiting room of Dr. Jerome's veterinary office. She still could not believe the events of the morning. Could this be real? How could she be here? Was she dreaming? Was she *really* going to fetch her precious Popsy and take her home?

After six weeks, Mamina had given up all hope of ever seeing her dear chaton ever again. That morning, she'd been seated at her kitchen table writing her list for the day. She'd gathered together the previous lists from that week so that she could make note of the tasks that were not yet complete and consolidate them all. Sipping her tea, she had clicked open her pen and begun the "to do" list for the day. She always found this to be a satisfying way to start the morning. Mamina felt best when she had a plan, when she knew what the day would hold and was able to work her way methodically though each task. It was always gratifying to sit at dinner in the evening with Papy Jean, knowing that she'd completed most if not all of the responsibilities she'd outlined for herself. Today had looked very straightforward, with nothing out of the ordinary. An easy day.

The phone had rung as she was standing to put her tea cup into the sink. A man's voice at the other end had inquired, "Bonjour, is this the home of Madame Denis?"

"Oui, I am Madame Denis."

"Madame, my name is Dr. Jerome. I am a veterinarian with an office in Versailles. I am calling to see if you have lost a cat—an exquisite tricolored female cat, one of the most beautiful and refined cats in the world. If so, I have the great pleasure to tell you that she has been found! I have her here in my office."

Sitting here in the waiting room, Mamina was still shaking her head in disbelief. He had her dear Popsy! Dr. Jerome had explained all about Madame Testoubay to Mamina on the phone. Oh Lord, what were the odds? How did Popsy get to Versailles? How long had she been here? How had she lived? So many questions! Mamina realized she'd never know the answers. But she would be happy just to have her dear, sweet chaton back again. Who would have ever thought this was possible?

The door to the examining room opened. Mamina looked over. There on the table was her dear Popsy! She could not believe her eyes. In that instant, Popsy stood up and meowed in her loudest voice, "Mamina! It is you! I am here! *Come get me!*" Mamina rushed in and scooped up her dear chaton in her arms. Popsy, who normally did not like being held all that much, immediately purred and rubbed her nose against Mamina's chin. Then she curled up and hunkered into the safety of her mother's embrace. Yes! Two best friends who had feared they'd lost each other forever were together again!

Night

HAT NIGHT, Popsy curled up into her favorite bed, the one with the patchwork design. She nestled into the perfect sleeping position, and purring softly, she closed her eyes, waiting for sleep to come. The lights were off, and the apartment was dark and quiet. She felt content and safe and at peace.

Just as she was drifting off, a rustling sound caught her attention. She opened one eye, just a slit, to see what was making the sound.

Shadows began to emerge from the hallway. One after the other, dark grey figures floated into the salon, and each took a seat on the sofa facing her. There was Dr. Jerome, Madame Testoubay, and even her cat, Melki. Oh my! Popsy began to purr as she watched the Sun King, Edgard Le Maître de la Glace, and Juliette the kitchen helper drift in and sit down. And, my goodness, Francois was there with Claudine! Even Pierre-Yves, the seafood truck driver, was there. All of them smiled, nodding their heads. None of them spoke.

Popsy raised her head and opened her eyes fully now. These were the companions who had traveled with her during her amazing journey. Each had helped to usher her along her way in one manner or another. With all of them gathered together like this, she felt like a circle had been completed.

She looked at each of them, one at a time. Then she stood, faced them and in her most solemn voice meowed, "I am home. I am safe. You each assisted me in your own way, even if you didn't know it. I am deeply grateful for your help and for this grand adventure. Thank you all so very much."

Dr. Jerome and Madame Testoubay (holding Melki) got up from their seats and walked over to her. They each gave her a gentle pat on the head. Then they slowly melted away into the air. One by one, each of Popsy's friends came to her and gave her a pat or a kiss goodbye and then disappeared. Finally just the king and Francois were left. They walked over, looked at each other, and then they both looked at Popsy. The king picked her up and gave her a long, warm hug. Then, kissing her on her head, he put her back into her bed. Francois was right there. He gave Popsy one long, loving lick with his tongue along her back. He rubbed his face against her nose. Then he and the Sun King slowly faded away.

Popsy sighed, and finally, she slept.

Fin

The Real Story

IN THE 1990'S THERE WAS A CAT NAMED POPSY who lived with Betsy's sister, Kathy Denis, in the 15th arrondissement of Paris. Kathy, who is called "Mamina" by her family, often allowed Popsy to play in the apartment's courtyard garden. One day in the spring of 2000 Popsy disappeared from the garden. All efforts to find her led nowhere, and as time passed Kathy feared the worst. But – six weeks later – Popsy actually did crawl through a cat door into someone's home in Versailles! At first, the kind woman from that house wondered if Popsy might be a weasel because she appeared so scrawny, tired and dirty. Then, realizing that the creature was not a weasel, but indeed a cat, she took Popsy to her veterinarian. Popsy had been registered with an ID, so the veterinarian was able to look up her name, call Kathy with the good news and they were reunited.

At the end of the previous December of 1999 there had been a catastrophic storm that blew down most if not all of the old oak trees on the Versailles estate. After that storm there truly were weasels in the streets of Versailles searching for food and shelter.

So – really – this all could be true, right?

ABOUT THE AUTHOR

As a computer skills instructor and technical editor of computer text-books for 25+ years, Betsy has written and edited thousands of pages of technical writing. This is her first foray into the world of fiction. Or at least it is the first time she's shared it with anyone! She lives in Santa Fe, New Mexico with her dog, three cats and one horse.

ABOUT THE ILLUSTRATOR

Leah Gonzales, a Colorado native, received her BFA at Maryland Institute College of Art, with a Major in Drawing and a Concentration in Illustration. She works in all mediums and has exhibited her fine art across the United states. She currently lives in San Francisco and works as a teacher with young children specializing in story telling. Besides making art daily, she enjoys taking walks, reading, and traveling. She hopes to one day go back to school to receive her MFA.

www.ingramcontent.com/pod-product-compliance
Lightning Source LLC
Chambersburg PA
CBHW031843170626
46807CB00004B/1591